PUFFIN BOOKS

CAPTAIN PUGWASH AND THE PIGWIG

That most unlikely of pirates, the greedy, selfish Captain Pugwash is at the helm once more. And his familiar crew – Barnabas, Willy, the Mate and Tom the cabin boy – are all aboard.

In these four adventures the crew turn vegetarian, their enemy Cut-throat Jake is defeated by a parrot, there's a fierce battle on the poop deck, and the pirates find a whole new way to walk the plank.

Captain Pugwash has been delighting readers for over thirty years, and all his fans, old and new, will revel in these new stories. John Ryan's text and drawings are as full of comic vigour as ever.

John Ryan was born in Edinburgh and spent much of his early life abroad and at boarding school in England. After war service in Burma he taught and then became a contributor to *Eagle* magazine, then in its infancy. Captain Pugwash, who later became his most famous creation on television and in picture books, was in fact created for *Eagle*. Other creations include Harris Tweed, Lettice Leefe, Mary, Mungo and Midge, and Sir Prancelot. John Ryan is married with three children and several grandchildren. He lives in Rye, Sussex, a one-time notorious haunt of smugglers and pirates.

Also by John Ryan

John Ryan

Captain Pugwash and the Pigwig

PUFFIN BOOKS

PUFFIN BOOKS

Published by the Penguin Group
Penguin Books Ltd, 27 Wrights Lane, London W8 5TZ, England
Penguin Books USA Inc., 375 Hudson Street, New York, New York 10014, USA
Penguin Books Australia Ltd, Ringwood, Victoria, Australia
Penguin Books Canada Ltd, 10 Alcorn Avenue, Toronto, Ontario, Canada M4V 3B2
Penguin Books (NZ) Ltd, 182–190 Wairau Road, Auckland 10, New Zealand

Penguin Books Ltd, Registered Offices: Harmondsworth, Middlesex, England

First published by Viking 1991
Published in Puffin Books 1993
10 9 8 7 6 5 4 3 2 1

Text and illustrations copyright © John Ryan, 1991
All rights reserved

The moral right of the author/illustrator has been asserted

Printed in England by Clays Ltd, St Ives plc
Filmset in Linotron Times

Contents

Captain
Pugwash and
the Pigwig

One day, while strolling through the market, Captain Pugwash saw a fat little suckling piglet for sale.

"That's *just* the thing to make me a delicious dinner when we set sail tomorrow," he thought.

So he bought it, and carried it back to his ship.

He felt very pleased with himself and could hardly wait for Tom the cabin boy to cook it next evening.

But no sooner had the ship set sail than the piglet escaped from the larder and started to make friends with the crew.

It could do all sorts of tricks.

 Like sitting
up and begging
for food,

and walking
on its front
trotters,

 and turning
somersaults.

Soon all the pirates became very fond of the piglet. They didn't at all want their Captain to have it for his dinner.

"We have all become vegetarian, Cap'n," said the Mate. "If you try to roast that there pig, there will be trouble, mark my words."

"Lay one finger on 'im, and we'll throw you to the sharks and the sea monsters," growled Pirate Barnabas.

"Aye! And sharks and sea monsters are NOT vegetarian!" added Pirate Willy.

13

"Fluttering flatfish," said Pugwash. "What a fuss about a fat little piglet!"

But there was nothing he could do. The crew named their new pet "Pigwig"

and the Captain had to watch them feeding him every kind of delicacy – out of *his* larder!

Then Pigwig
started to grow.

He got bigger
and fatter,

and bigger
and fatter,
until he
wasn't a piglet any more . . .

but a huge great porker!

Then the crew decided that
Pigwig needed more
comfortable quarters.

So he
had his meals at the Captain's
table,

and slept in the Captain's bunk.

Poor Captain Pugwash. There
was very little room left for
him, and it soon became rather
smelly in his cabin.

In fact, all over the ship,

the pirates were having to hold
their noses.

Another problem was that as
Pigwig grew bigger, so did his
appetite.

The ship's food supplies were
beginning to run low –

and the crew began to wonder
whether their pet *was* such a
good thing after all.

Then Tom the
cabin boy,
who had been
keeping very
quiet, called
out, "Look!

There's an island over there!

Let's go ashore and see if
there's any food."

"Good idea, Tom lad," said
the Mate. "Man the longboat,
Shipmates!"

So they dropped anchor and
the crew rowed ashore in the
longboat.

The island was full of trees
and shrubs covered with fruit
and berries and nuts. Just what
the pirates were looking for.

21

Soon they were on their
way back, with baskets full
of goodies.

Then Tom
steered the
ship far
away from
the island.

Meanwhile, Captain Pugwash and the pirates settled down to the biggest and best meal they had had for a long time. It was only when they were beginning to feel really full and rather sleepy that the Mate remarked:

"That's werry peculiar! I don't see our Pigwig nowhere!"

"You're right . . . 'ee's gone!" cried Barnabas.

"Pig overboard!" called Willy, running to the side.

But Tom smiled. "Don't worry," he said. "I rowed

Pigwig ashore in the dinghy while you were looking for food.

I left him there. He's far better off with his own kind."

Tom was right. On the island, Pigwig had already met lots of interesting gentlemen pigs, and attractive lady pigs. He was very happy indeed. His new companions were much more fun than the pirates!

On board the ship the crew were happy too. In fact, they danced with joy because now there was plenty to eat . . .

and it wasn't anything like so smelly!

Only Captain Pugwash wasn't quite as pleased as everybody else.

After all, he had never had
that delicious dinner he had so
looked forward to at the start
of the voyage!

Captain
Pugwash and
the Parrot

It was the Captain's birthday,
and his crew wanted to give
him a present.

They thought of an
eye-patch, but that reminded
them of their worst enemy,
Cut-throat Jake. They thought
of a wooden leg, but
remembered that Pugwash
already had two perfectly good
legs.

So, in the end, they decided on a parrot.

"Every pirate should have one," said the Mate.

"Ar . . . and they come cheap round here," said Barnabas.

So, as the ship was in harbour, they went ashore and bought the least expensive parrot they could find.

"Happy Birthday, dear Cap'n," sang all the pirates together as they gave Pugwash his present.

"Happy Birthday!" sang the parrot . . . and bit the Captain on the nose.

"Ouch! . . . er, yes, er, well . . . thank you very much," said Pugwash. He wasn't very fond of birds, and had already taken a strong dislike to this one.

"I take it," he said, as he stuck a plaster on to his nose, "that you have bought a *cage* for the creature?"

"No cage,
Cap'n," said
the Mate.

"Money ran
out," said
Barnabas.

"Christmas is
coming," said
Willy.

34

"You'll have to keep it in
your cabin, Cap'n," said the
Mate,

and because he didn't want to
hurt the crew's feelings,
Captain Pugwash agreed.

So Tom the
cabin boy, who
seemed to get along quite well
with the parrot, took it

and made it comfortable in the
Captain's cabin.

But sadly, right from the start,

the birthday present was
not a success.

The parrot snapped at its
new owner

whenever Pugwash came within
reach . . .

and also started to imitate the Captain in a very rude manner.

It took to repeating his favourite sayings, like "What-ho, me hearties!" or "Shuddering sharks!" or "Jumping jellyfish!".

What ho, me hearties!

Shuddering Sharks!

Jumping Jellyfish!

Sometimes it shouted out
orders in the Captain's voice,
like "Splice the mainbrace!",
which means "Free rum for
all!".

This made the crew, who
loved their rum, very happy,
and the Captain, who was as
mean as anything, very cross.

But the parrot did worse than that. Every day after lunch, the Captain liked to take a little snooze.

When he snoozed, he snored.

And when he snored, the parrot imitated his snoring.

He did it so cleverly that
nobody could tell the difference.

The parrot's snoring became
so loud that

the Captain couldn't sleep at
night, let alone after lunch!

One afternoon, Pugwash got fed up with trying to sleep. So he decided to take a walk into town with the crew.

Little did he realize that his enemy, Cut-throat Jake, was lurking near by and planning a raid on the *Black Pig*.

In fact, that very afternoon, thinking that the Captain would be asleep as usual, Jake sneaked up the gangplank,

across the deck,

and along to the Captain's cabin.

The only person in sight was
Tom the cabin boy, and for
once Tom seemed quite
friendly.

"Looking for the Cap'n?"
Tom asked. "Listen!"

Then, with his ear to the Captain's door, Jake heard the Captain's voice.

"Battling barnacles! It's my bedtime!" said the voice, and there followed a lot of loud snoring.

"Ha-harrh! . . . asleep, eh? . . . caught like a lobster in a pot," breathed Jake.

Waving his cutlass, he rushed into the cabin.

The Captain wasn't there, of course . . . but the parrot was! It took one look at the intruder, and went for him!

Cut-throat Jake was a
savage fighter, but he was no
match for the parrot!

Pecked and scratched
and bitten, he fled in terror
out of the cabin,

47

off the ship,

and away down the quayside.

And that was what Captain
Pugwash and his crew saw as
they strolled back to the *Black
Pig*.

48

"Well, well, well," said Pugwash, "it's that old villain, Cut-throat Jake.

We shan't see *him* again for a while, by the look of it!"

"Nor," he added to himself with a happy smile,

"my birthday parrot!"

Captain Pugwash and the Plank

It was a very very hot day. The
Black Pig was becalmed in the
Caribbean sea. The Mate,
Willy and Barnabas were lying
about on deck, snoozing and
sunbathing and doing nothing
very much.

52

Even Tom the cabin boy, who
usually did all the hard work,
was reading a book in a shady
corner.

Captain Pugwash wasn't
doing much either. He had just
eaten a very large lunch. Now
he was sleeping it off
peacefully in his cabin.

As he slept, the Captain began
to dream . . .

. . . and his dream was
anything but peaceful!

He dreamed that his crew were fed up with him. So much so that they had decided they didn't need a Captain any more and could run the ship by themselves.

"Help! This is mutiny!" thought Pugwash in his dream.

Worse was to come.
   "Let's get rid of him altogether!" said the Mate.

"Ar!" put in Willy. "Who wants an extra mouth to feed?"

"Tell you what," chuckled Barnabas, "let's make 'im walk the plank . . . and make an end of 'im!"

Then all the pirates cheered, and even Tom, his faithful cabin boy, started to fix up the plank.

Poor Captain Pugwash! His dream was fast turning into a nightmare!

For now the pirates were
pushing him out along the
plank.

"Jump for it, Cap'n!"
shouted the
Mate. "Or
we'll blow
you off
with the
cannon!"

The Captain jumped. He fell
and he fell and he fell . . . and
he landed . . .

with a bump

. . . wide awake on the floor of his cabin. He had fallen out of his bunk and woken up.

"Whew!" breathed Captain Pugwash. "What a relief! It was only a bad dream!"

60

But then he heard a noise
outside on the deck. It was a
hammering noise. It was just
like the hammering noise he
had heard in his dream, when
Tom was nailing down the
plank. So he peeped out on
deck . . .

and "OH NO!!" he
muttered.

"It's TRUE!!" For there was
Tom the cabin boy,

and he really *was* nailing a
plank to the deck! The Mate
and Barnabas stood around
watching him gleefully.

"Tottering turtles! This is truly terrible!" thought the Captain.

"There really *is* a mutiny going on! There's only one thing to do . . . escape . . . before they come for me and make me walk the plank!"

Quickly he put on his coat
and his boots. He packed a
basket full of food
and water
and a flask
of rum.

He stuffed a small treasure-
chest with all
the gold and
silver and jewels
that he kept
hidden in his
cabin.

It was quite a job to shut it because he couldn't bear to leave anything behind. Then he carried everything stealthily

out of his cabin and along to the far end of the *Black Pig*, where the dinghy was kept.

He loaded all his precious things into the little boat, and was just about to lower it very very quietly over the side, when he heard Tom calling him.

"What on earth are you doing messing about with the dinghy?" cried the cabin boy. "We're all going to have a swim and cool off!

I've just fixed up a DIVING-BOARD! Come on!"

"Oh, there you are, Cap'n!" called the Mate as Pugwash and Tom arrived. "Come and join us!"

The pirates were all dressed in their swimming things.

"You go first, Tom lad!" said Barnabas. "Show us how to do it!"

So Tom ran along the plank
and did quite a neat
swallow-dive.

He hardly
made any
splash as
he entered
the water.

Willy went next. He did a honey-pot and made quite a splash.

Barnabas tried a back-dive and made a very big splash.

The Mate did a belly-flop and made a very big splash indeed.

But Captain Pugwash did a back-front double somersault, with a special sideways twist . . . and made the biggest splash

of the lot! He was so happy to find that the plank was only a diving-board after all.

He even managed to keep
his hat on!

Captain
Pugwash and
the Poop Deck

"All hands to the poop deck, Master Mate!" cried Captain Pugwash. "Fluttering flounders! It's absolutely filthy up here. High time the deck was given a good scrubbing!"

"Aye, aye, Cap'n," grunted the Mate sleepily.

74

"Come on, look sharp,
Barnabas and Willy! All hands
to the poop
deck!"

Barnabas was fishing and
Willy was playing skittles.
Neither of them was in any
hurry to obey
the Mate's
command.

"Wot is a poop deck, anyway?" grumbled Willy, as he set to work.

"Really, Pirate William," said Captain Pugwash. "How long have you been at sea?

The poop deck is the highest
deck at the stern, or back end,
of the ship, of course!

On it is the steering-wheel,
and there stands the most
important person aboard . . .
the Captain himself . . . *me*!"
  "When 'ee's not asleep in 'is
cabin," muttered Barnabas.
But the Captain pretended not
to hear.

77

"And," he went on, "by
far the bravest, most
handsome buccaneer . . ."
But suddenly the
Captain was rudely
interrupted.

"I'll give 'ee brave an' 'andsome!!" snarled a ferocious voice behind him.

There, to everybody's horror, was Cut-throat Jake, the Captain's worst enemy. Silently, he had climbed up the stern of the ship.

Now he leaped over the rail, on to the deck and roared:

"Come on, you old scallywag Pugwash! Draw your sword! We'll soon see who's the bravest an' most 'andsome."

The crew were terrified. A
few seconds later, there
wasn't one
of them
of them
to be seen.
They had
all slipped
away from the poop

deck to a
place from
which they
could watch

without
being seen.

Even Tom the
cabin boy had
disappeared,
though nobody
quite knew
where.

But most frightened of all
was Captain Pugwash.

For all his boasting, he was no
good at fighting at all! He was
certainly no match for
Cut-throat Jake.

"Help!" cried Pugwash,

as his deadly enemy chased
him up and down the poop
deck, slashing at him with his
enormous cutlass.

In vain, the Captain tried to dodge round the steering-wheel. He tried to escape up the rigging.

But Jake cut him down again.

He tried to jump over the
side, but Jake pulled him
back again.

Then he knocked the sword
out of Pugwash's
hand,

and tied him
up with his own rope.

From a safe distance, the crew watched while Cut-throat Jake strode up and down, waving his cutlass in triumph and stroking his huge black beard.

"That'll teach 'im to tell us to scrub decks," muttered Barnabas.

"Looks like we've got a new Cap'n," whispered Willy.

"Oh dear!" said the Mate.

Willy was right.

"Ha-ha-harhh!!" roared Cut-throat Jake. "The vessel is mine – all mine, an' I'll sail her to my own home port!"

And he seized the wheel with his great hairy hands and began to turn the ship.

But what Jake had not
realized was that he was
standing on a hatchway,

and that in the sail-locker
underneath,

Tom the cabin boy was busy
undoing the bolt.

Suddenly, in the middle of a
roar of triumphant laughter,
Cut-throat Jake found himself
falling through the poop deck,
into the sail-locker below.

Quick as a flash, Tom climbed up through the hatchway

. . . pulled it tight shut . . .

and lashed it to the base of the
steering-wheel with some rope.

Jake was imprisoned and very
uncomfortable. He swore
horribly, but there was nothing
he could do about it, and there
he stayed for the rest of the
voyage.

So the *Black Pig* continued
on her way . . .

with Captain Pugwash at the
wheel. He was even more
pleased with himself than ever.

"Poor old Cut-throat Jake," he boasted to the crew. "His wicked plots always fall through – HA HA – in the end!

And as for all of you – I hope you will always remember what a poop deck is: the place where the most important person on board is always to be found!"

"Hmm," thought Tom. "If you ask me, *our* poop deck is a place where you find silly old poops!"

But he just smiled . . . and said nothing.